Little One

JO WEAVER

PEACHTREE
ATLANTA

Big Bear stepped out of her winter den.

By her side, half asleep and blinking in the spring sunshine,

wobbled a tiny cub.

"There's so much to discover in your new world,

Little One," said Big Bear.

She led her cub to the forest, where new life

was stirring among the trees.

"This is where our journey begins," she said.

Big Bear showed Little One how

to be gentle with friends…

and how to enjoy the long summer days.

Little One watched Big Bear and learned how to fish…

and how to swim safely in the cool forest lake.

"I'm with you, Little One," said Big Bear.

Together they explored far and wide…

and filled their hungry tummies

with ripe autumn berries.

Little One played in the blustery wind.

But Big Bear felt restless.

She knew that winter was coming.

It began to snow and as cold flakes settled on the ground,

Big Bear led their way out of the forest.

Together they

climbed up the hillside.

For a moment, they stopped

to look back at their land,

now covered in snow.

The wind roared and the snow piled high,

but Big Bear found their old den...

and it smelled of home.

In the warm darkness, Big Bear and Little One

curled up together and waited for spring.

For Mum and Dad,
who read to me then…
and for Dom,
who reads to me now
—*J. W.*

Published by
PEACHTREE PUBLISHERS
1700 Chattahoochee Avenue
Atlanta, Georgia 30318-2112
www.peachtree-online.com

Text and illustrations © 2016 by Jo Weaver

First published in Great Britain in 2016
by Hodder Children's Books
First United States version published in 2016
by Peachtree Publishers

Illustrations rendered in charcoal

Printed in 2015 in China
10 9 8 7 6 5 4 3 2 1
First Edition
ISBN 978-1-56145-924-7 (hardcover)
ISBN 978-1-56145-925-4 (trade paperback)

Cataloging-in-Publication Data is available
from the Library of Congress